Titles in the series...

Graphic Chillers
DRACULA
EDGE
Bram Stoker • Daniel Conner • Rod Espinosa

Graphic Chillers
FRANKENSTEIN
EDGE
Mary Shelley • Elizabeth Genco • Jason Ho

EDGE
H.G. Wells • Joeming Dunn • Ben Dunn

Graphic Chillers
DR. & MR. JEKYLL HYDE
EDGE
Robert Louis Stevenson • Jason Ho

Graphic Chillers
THE LEGEND OF SLEEPY HOLLOW
EDGE
Washington Irving • Jeff Zornow

Graphic Chillers
MUMMY
EDGE
Bram Stoker • Bart A. Thompson • Brian Miroglio

Graphic Chillers
THE PHANTOM OF THE OPERA
EDGE
Gaston Leroux • Joeming Dunn • Rod Espinosa

Graphic Chillers
WEREWOLF
EDGE
Jeff Zornow

THE PHANTOM OF THE OPERA

ABOUT THE AUTHOR

Gaston Leroux was born in Paris, France, on 6 May, 1868. After leaving school he worked in a law office. He also began writing essays and stories.

By 1890, Leroux was working full-time as a journalist. He travelled the world from 1894 to 1906, reporting back to Paris. He also began writing novels. In 1907, his first success was *The Mystery of the Yellow Room*. Leroux wrote several books based on the main character, but none were as successful.

In 1911, *The Phantom of the Opera* was published. It received poor reviews and did not sell very well. Leroux continued to write and published several novels and plays, but he did not receive much recognition until 1925, when *The Phantom of the Opera* was turned into a silent movie starring American actor Lon Chaney.

Gaston Leroux died in April 1927 in France. He did not become famous in his lifetime. However, *The Phantom of the Opera* became widely known after Andrew Lloyd Webber's musical adaption in 1986.

Graphic Chillers

THE PHANTOM OF THE OPERA

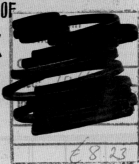

ADAPTED BY
JOEMING DUNN

ILLUSTRATED BY
ROD ESPINOSA

BASED UPON THE WORKS OF
GASTON LEROUX

EDGE
FRANKLIN WATTS

LONDON·SYDNEY

THE PHANTOM OF THE OPERA

"I WAS *CURSED* THE DAY I WAS BORN. I WAS SO *UGLY* MY MOTHER NEVER KISSED ME. I WAS NOT A CHILD BUT A *MONSTER*."

"WHEN I WAS OLDER, I JOINED A *FREAK SHOW*. I TRAVELLED FAR AND WIDE SINGING AND PERFORMING MAGIC."

WHAT IS YOUR NAME?

I AM ERIK.

"ONE NIGHT A PERSIAN VISITED AND INVITED ME TO LIVE LIKE A KING WITH THE SHAH OF PERSIA."

"WHILE IN PERSIA, I ENTERTAINED THE SHAH. I BUILT MANY SECRET PASSAGES IN THE PALACE FOR MY MAGIC TRICKS."

"SOON, THE SHAH FEARED I KNEW TOO MUCH AND ORDERED MY DEATH."

"BUT THE PERSIAN TOOK PITY ON ME. HE HELPED ME ESCAPE TO PARIS, AND I TOOK REFUGE IN A NEW OPERA HOUSE."

"THE MANAGERS OF THE OPERA HOUSE WERE MESSIEURS DEBIENNE AND POLIGNY. THEY LET ME STAY THERE FOR MANY YEARS. THEN THEY PREPARED TO RETIRE."

SOME OF THE OPERA'S DANCERS WERE TALKING ABOUT A GHOST.

JOSEPH BUQUET, THE CHIEF SCENE SHIFTER, HAS SEEN THE *PHANTOM.*

HIS DRESS COAT HANGS ON A *SKELETON FRAME.*

HIS EYES ARE SO *DEEP* YOU SEE TWO, BIG BLACK HOLES JUST LIKE IN A *DEAD MAN'S SKULL.*

WELL, YOU KNOW ABOUT THE GHOST'S *PRIVATE BOX?*

WHAT BOX?

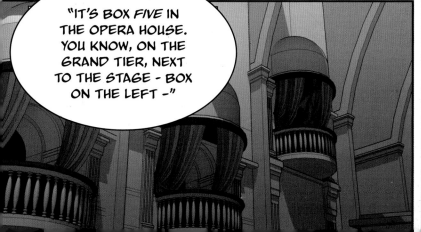

"IT'S BOX *FIVE* IN THE OPERA HOUSE. YOU KNOW, ON THE GRAND TIER, NEXT TO THE STAGE - BOX ON THE LEFT -"

BUQUET *IS DEAD!* HE WAS FOUND IN THE THIRD-FLOOR CELLAR!

IT MUST BE THE *PHANTOM!*

THAT EVENING WAS CHRISTINE DAAE'S GREATEST MOMENT. SHE WAS PLAYING MARGARITA IN THE OPERA *FAUST* FOR THE FIRST TIME.

CARLOTTA, THE PREVIOUS LEADING LADY, HAD *MYSTERIOUSLY* FALLEN 'ILL'. THE WHOLE THING WAS OVERWHELMING FOR CHRISTINE.

IN THE AUDIENCE WERE TWO ARISTOCRATS, RAOUL AND HIS BROTHER PHILIPPE DE CHAGNY.

CHRISTINE IS *FAINTING*.

YOU LOOK LIKE FAINTING YOURSELF.

LET'S GO AND SEE HER.

MONSIEUR, WHO ARE *YOU*?

YOU MUST REMEMBER ME. I AM THE LITTLE BOY WHO RESCUED YOUR SCARF.

I SHOULD LIKE TO SAY SOMETHING IN *PRIVATE*, SOMETHING VERY IMPORTANT.

WHEN I AM BETTER, DO YOU MIND? EXCUSE ME, I SHOULD LIKE TO BE *ALONE*. PLEASE GO AWAY.

PLEASE GO, ALL OF YOU.

RAOUL HID AS CHRISTINE LEFT.

THERE IS SOMEONE HERE! WHY ARE YOU *HIDING*?

IF YOU DON'T ANSWER, YOU ARE A *COWARD*! BUT I'LL EXPOSE YOU!

WHAT'S THAT?

THAT IS JOSEPH BUQUET. HE WAS FOUND DEAD IN THE CELLAR.

14

SUDDENLY THE CHANDELIER FELL, AND THE MANAGERS HEARD A VOICE SAY, "SHE IS SINGING TONIGHT TO BRING THE CHANDELIER DOWN!"

ERIK TOOK CHRISTINE THROUGH SECRET PASSAGES TO AN UNDERGROUND LAKE.

WHO ARE YOU?

I AM ERIK, DO NOT BE AFRAID. YOU ARE NOT IN DANGER.

YOU... YOU ARE THE ANGEL OF MUSIC! YOU ARE JUST A MAN!

AS THEY SANG, LOVE, JEALOUSY AND HATRED FILLED THE AIR.

SUDDENLY, CHRISTINE FELT A NEED TO SEE BENEATH THE MASK. SHE *WANTED* TO KNOW THE FACE OF THE VOICE, AND, WITH ONE MOVEMENT, SHE *TORE* AWAY THE MASK.

HORROR!
HORROR!
HORROR!

I AM HIDEOUS.

NO... NO... YOUR FACE DOES NOT MATTER. YOU ARE THE ANGEL OF MUSIC.

CHRISTINE STAYED UNDERGROUND BUT FREELY MOVED ABOUT THE MANY HIDDEN ROOMS.

ONE DAY, ERIK MET A FAMILIAR FACE IN THE CELLARS. IT WAS THE PERSIAN.

WHAT ARE YOU DOING HERE?

I HEARD THAT A YOUNG SINGER IS *MISSING*. DO YOU KNOW WHERE SHE IS?

SHE IS WITH ME IN MY HOUSE.

YOU MUST LET HER GO.

SHE IS IN LOVE WITH ME. I CAN *PROVE* IT AT THE MASKED BALL TOMORROW NIGHT.

AGREED.

19

THROUGH THE MANY SECRET PASSAGES, DOORS, LADDERS AND BRIDGES, THE COUPLE RACED UP TO THE ROOF.

BEHIND THE TRAPDOOR THEY FOUND DARK PASSAGES AND TUNNELS.

FINALLY, THEY REACHED A DAMP ROOM COVERED IN MIRRORS.

CHRISTINE! CHRISTINE!

RAOUL!

CHRISTINE! CAN YOU LET US OUT?

I DO NOT HAVE A KEY.

THE *PHANTOM* HAS GIVEN ME UNTIL ELEVEN O'CLOCK TO MARRY HIM. IF I SAY NO, *EVERYBODY* WILL BE BURIED UNDER THE RUINS OF THE OPERA HOUSE.

ERIK EXPLAINED HOW HE SAVED THEM FROM THEIR WATERY GRAVES. HE HAD TORN OFF HIS MASK AND SHE REMAINED, WEEPING.

CHRISTINE, *SWEAR* TO COME BACK ONE NIGHT AND *BURY* ME WITH THE GOLD RING.

IF CHRISTINE KEEPS HER PROMISE, SHE WILL COME BACK SOON!

GO TO THE OPERA.

THREE WEEKS LATER...

ERIK IS DEAD

This edition first published in 2010 by
Franklin Watts
338 Euston Road
London NW1 3BH

Franklin Watts Australia
Level 17/207 Kent Street
Sydney NSW 2000

First published in the USA by Magic Wagon, a division of the ABDO Group

1 3 5 7 9 10 8 6 4 2

Original novel by Gaston Leroux
Adapted by Joeming Dunn
Illustrated, coloured and lettered by Rod Espinosa
Edited by Stephanie Hedlund and Rochelle Baltzer
Interior layout and design by Antarctic Press
Cover art by Ben Dunn
Original cover design by Neil Klinepier
UK cover design by Peter Scoulding

A CIP catalogue record for this book is available from the British Library.

Dewey number: 741.5

ISBN: 978 0 7496 9682 5

Printed in China

Franklin Watts is a division of Hachette Children's Books,
an Hachette UK company.
www.hachette.co.uk